Weekly Reader Books presents

BARKLEY
by Syd Hoff

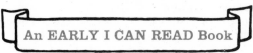
An EARLY I CAN READ Book

HARPER & ROW, PUBLISHERS
New York, Evanston, San Francisco, London

This book is a presentation of Weekly Reader Books.
Weekly Reader Books offers book clubs for children
from preschool through high school. For further
information write to: **Weekly Reader Books,**
4343 Equity Drive, Columbus, Ohio 43228.

Published by arrangement with
Harper & Row, Publishers, Inc.

BARKLEY

Library of Congress Catalog Card Number: 75-6290
Trade Standard Book Number: 06–022447–9
Harpercrest Standard Book Number: 06–022448–7

For Francesca Manushkin

Barkley had a job

in the circus.

He did tricks with

four other dogs.

Barkley walked on his front legs.

He walked on his back legs.

The other dogs

stood on Barkley's back

and jumped off.

If one of the dogs

did something wrong,

Barkley barked!

Barkley always led the way

when they walked on a rope.

Everyone clapped and cheered,

and Barkley took a bow.

8

Then he played

with the children.

Barkley liked that best of all.

But one day,

when the four dogs

jumped on Barkley's back,

it hurt!

Another day,

Barkley walked too slowly.

The other dogs went ahead of him.

"I will be all right,"

thought Barkley.

But he was too tired

to take a bow.

12

"I think you are getting old,"
said Barkley's owner.
"That happens to all of us."

The next day,

Barkley's owner said,

"I don't want you to get hurt.

Another dog

is taking your place."

Barkley saw the other dog

doing his tricks.

He did them very well.

Barkley missed the clapping,
and he missed the cheering.
But he missed the children
most of all.

"There must be *something*
I can do," he thought.
Barkley tried to work
with the seals.
But the ball would not stay
on his nose.

17

He tried to do tricks

with the elephants.

But he only got in their way.

18

Barkley joined the act
on the flying trapeze.
But when he flew
through the air,
nobody caught him!

19

"I guess there is nothing

I can do here," he thought.

So when nobody was looking,

Barkley left the circus.

He walked and walked
for a long time.

Barkley was tired and hungry.

"If I do a trick,"

he thought, "maybe someone

will give me a bone."

He walked on his front legs.

He walked on his back legs.

Nobody gave him a bone.

GARBAGE

He saw a bone

in a garbage can.

But someone came

and took it away.

24

"Nobody likes
an old circus dog,"
thought Barkley.
He went into a yard to rest.

Children were playing there!

Barkley was so happy

he did some tricks for them.

The children played with him,

and they gave him food and water.

They liked Barkley so much

they wanted to keep him.

"We cannot keep you,"

said a girl.

"There is only one place

for a smart dog like you."

She took Barkley

back to the circus!

"Where were you?"

asked his owner.

"I missed you."

"I didn't want you

to leave the circus.

We need you to teach

young dogs your tricks."

Barkley was very happy!

He began his new job the next day.

Barkley showed his tricks

to the young dogs.

When a dog

did something wrong,

Barkley barked.

Now Barkley had more time

to play with the children.

And he never

left the circus again!